Praise for The Imagination Station® books

Challenge on the Hill of Fire is a great story of courage. It will help kids stay strong in their faith.

—Tamra B., mother of two
Chino, California

These books are a great combination of history and adventure in a clean manner perfect for young children.

—Margie B., *My Springfield Mommy* blog

Readers of *Challenge on the Hill of Fire* will find their faith in God strengthened as they follow cousins Patrick and Beth on an exciting adventure. . . . What begins as a "green" day ends up as a story about Saint Patrick and his vision of sharing the gospel around the world.

—Colleen C., second-grade teacher
Chino Hills, California

More praise for *The Imagination Station*® *books*

My nine-year-old son has already read [the first two books], one of them twice. He is very eager to read more in the series too. I am planning on reading them out loud to my younger son.

—Abbi C., mother of four, Minnesota

[The Imagination Station books] focus on God much more than the Magic Tree House books do.

—Emilee, age 7, Waynesboro, Pennsylvania

Our children have been riveted and on the edge of their seats through each and every chapter of The Imagination Station books. The series is well-written, engaging, family-friendly, and has great spiritual truths woven into the stories. Highly recommended!

—Crystal P., *Money Saving Mom*®

FOCUS ON THE FAMILY PRESENTS

THE IMAGINATION STATION

Challenge on the Hill of Fire

BOOK 10

MARIANNE HERING • NANCY I. SANDERS
CREATIVE DIRECTION BY PAUL McCUSKER
ILLUSTRATED BY DAVID HOHN

TYNDALE

FOCUS ON THE FAMILY • ADVENTURES IN ODYSSEY
TYNDALE HOUSE PUBLISHERS, INC. • CAROL STREAM, ILLINOIS

Challenge on the Hill of Fire

© 2012 Focus on the Family. All rights reserved.

ISBN: 978-1-58997-694-8

A Focus on the Family book published by Tyndale House Publishers, Inc., Carol Stream, Illinois 60188

The Imagination Station, Adventures in Odyssey, and *Focus on the Family* and the accompanying logo and design are federally registered trademarks of Focus on the Family, 8605 Explorer Drive, Colorado Springs, CO 80920.

TYNDALE and Tyndale's quill logo are registered trademarks of Tyndale House Publishers, Inc.

With the exception of known historical figures, all characters are the product of the authors' imaginations.

Cover design by Michael Heath | Magnus Creative

Cataloging-in-Publication Data for this book is available by contacting the Library of Congress at http://www.loc.gov/help/contact-general.html.

For information about special discounts for bulk purchases, please contact Tyndale House Publishers at csresponse@tyndale.com, or call 1-800-323-9400.

Printed in the United States of America

25 24 23 22 21 20 19
12 11 10   9   8   7   6

To Ben and Christina,

By the time this book comes out, you'll be married

and starting a new life together. Just imagine! Each

new day will be as exciting as going on an adventure

in the Imagination Station. Dad and I thank God

for both of you!

—NIS

Contents

A Leprechaun Trap

Patrick and his cousin Beth stood in line at Whit's End. It was Odyssey's most popular ice-cream shop.

Patrick felt very excited. Today was a special day. He was dressed in green. He wore a green baseball cap and a green T-shirt. He had on green shorts, green socks, and a pair of green sneakers.

Beth wore a green shamrock pin on her shirt.

Mr. Whittaker stood
behind the counter. He
finished with one customer and then
turned to Patrick and Beth. His kind blue
eyes sparkled. He lightly touched his large
white moustache.

"Hi, Patrick . . . Beth. What
can I do for you?" he asked.

"Beth and I would both
like a green milkshake,
please," Patrick
said. "We're
celebrating
Saint
Patrick's Day
today!"
Whit

touched his light-green shirt. "So am I," he said with a smile. He began making the milkshakes. He glanced at Patrick. "Were you named after Saint Patrick?" he asked.

"I don't think so," Patrick said. "I think I was named after my Uncle Patrick."

"But you know about Saint Patrick, I assume," Whit said.

Patrick looked at Beth. She shrugged.

"He wore green, right?" Patrick guessed.

Whit chuckled. "There was more to Saint Patrick than a color," he said.

"What do you mean?" Beth asked.

Whit's eyes twinkled. "I'll tell you more when I bring the milkshakes to your table."

Patrick and Beth sat down at one of the tables to wait. They watched Whit fill their orders.

Just then the door opened. Patrick's neighbor Jake walked in. He wore a yellow bandana tied around his neck. He had on his Cub Scout cap. His Cub T-shirt was green.

Patrick liked going over to Jake's house. That's where they met for their Cub Scout meetings.

"Happy Saint Patrick's Day!" Patrick and Beth both said to Jake.

Jake waved to the cousins and stood in line to order. Then he walked over to their table. He was carrying a bag. He had just bought freshly baked cookies.

"Are you going to eat all those cookies by yourself?" Patrick asked.

"Some friends are coming over to my house in a few minutes," Jake said. "We're going to build a leprechaun trap. I want to catch a leprechaun. Then he'll have to give us a pot of gold. We'll be rich!"

"Are you using the cookies as bait?" Beth asked.

Jake looked at the bag. "I hadn't thought of that," he said. "Do leprechauns like chocolate-chip cookies?"

"They might if leprechauns existed," Beth said. "But they *don't*."

"Come over and see for yourself," Jake said. He headed for the door. "Hurry up! You don't want to miss your share of the gold." The bell above the door jingled as it shut behind him.

Beth's eyebrows drew together in a frown. "A leprechaun trap? *Really*?" she asked.

Patrick smiled. "Maybe we'll catch one.

Wouldn't that be cool?"

Mr. Whittaker arrived with their orders. "What's all this about leprechauns?" he asked.

"Beth and I are going to help build a leprechaun trap with Jake," Patrick said.

Whit sat down. "Are you?" he asked. "Well, I hope you use the right kind of wood and nails. You can't make a trap out of just anything, you know."

Patrick's eyes lit up. "Maybe you should write out the instructions," he said.

Whit laughed. He had a deep, hearty laugh.

Beth groaned. She said, "I don't understand what all this has to do with Saint Patrick. He wasn't a leprechaun."

Whit looked at Beth and then Patrick.

"Would you like to find out?" he asked.

Patrick and Beth looked at each other. That question usually meant one thing: an adventure in the Imagination Station. The Imagination Station was one of Whit's many inventions. It allowed kids to experience different times in history.

"Can we?" Patrick asked.

Beth clapped her hands together. "Sure!" she said.

Patrick suddenly shook his head. "Wait a minute," he said. "I mean, what if it's true? What if we could get a pot of gold?"

"What?" Beth cried out. "When have you ever heard reports of any leprechaun sightings in Odyssey?"

Patrick frowned and said, "I still don't want to miss building a trap with Jake and the group. We've got to get going."

"You know how the Imagination Station works," Whit said. "Time is different there. I think you'll be able to have an adventure and still build leprechaun traps if you want to. Besides, the treasure you'll find in your adventure may be better than a pot of gold."

"Really?" Patrick asked. He was doubtful.

"Come down to the workshop and find out for yourself," Whit said.

The Gifts

Whit's workshop was in the basement of Whit's End. Whit worked on most of his inventions there.

The Imagination Station sat in the middle of the large room. The machine had a round front with dark glass and a door on each side. Patrick thought it looked like the front of a helicopter.

Whit touched a button on the side of the machine. The door facing them slid open.

Patrick waited for Beth to climb in. Then he slid onto the seat next to her.

"Wait," Whit said. He reached over to a worktable and picked up a small tin box. He handed it to Patrick.

Patrick held it up. It was small enough to fit in the palm of his hand.

"A tin of breath mints?" Beth asked.

Patrick suddenly smiled. "I know what this is! It's a flint and tinderbox."

"You're right!" Whit said. He sounded impressed.

Patrick opened the box. Inside were a small flat rock, a little bar of steel, and a piece of charred cloth.

"This is how

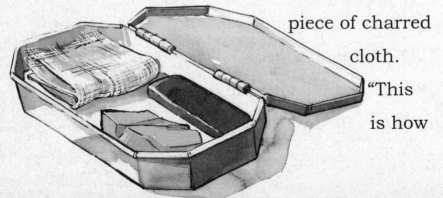

they started fires before matches were invented," he said to Beth.

Beth turned to Whit. "Do you have anything for me to take?" she asked.

Whit reached into his left pocket. He pulled out two acorns and handed them to Beth. "These will be used when someone's in great danger," he said. "You'll need to take action quickly."

Beth looked at the acorns. "He gets to start fires, and I get to . . . plant trees?" she asked.

Whit smiled at her. "You'll see when the time comes," he said.

The Imagination Station began to hum loudly. The lights on the dashboard in front of Patrick flashed.

"Just push the red button when you're ready," Whit said.

Beth nodded to Patrick. He pushed the red button.

As the door closed, Patrick heard Whit's voice. It sounded as if he were far away.

"Beware of the druids!" Whit called out. "But look for the bishop. He'll help you!"

"Druids?" Beth asked Patrick in the growing darkness.

Patrick didn't have time to answer. The Imagination Station shook and rattled. It rumbled. It rocked back and forth.

Then everything went dark.

Kidnapped!

Oink. Oink. Grunt. Oink!

Beth and Patrick stood in the mud. The Imagination Station faded away.

Black, brown, and spotted pigs crowded all around them. The pigs dug in the mud with their snouts. They oinked and squealed.

Beth looked at Patrick's clothes and pointed. "Look at you," she said.

The Imagination Station had altered their clothes.

Patrick was now dressed in a red tunic that reached down to his knees. Beneath that he wore a pair of brown leggings. A striped cape hung from his shoulders. It was clasped over his right shoulder with a metal brooch. A wide belt was wrapped around his waist. The tinderbox was inside the pocket of his tunic.

Beth wore a long white dress with sleeves. Over that she had on a bright-blue vest that laced down the front and a long purple skirt that reached to the ground. She put her hands in the pockets. The two acorns were inside one of the pockets.

Beth wrinkled her nose. "This place stinks," she said.

Patrick sniffed. "P.U., I think we stink too," he said.

Beth shivered. "*Brrrr.* I'm freezing," she said.

"Me, too," Patrick said. He rubbed his arms with his hands.

A cold, wet fog hung over everything. It was hard to see. Beth heard the sound of running water.

At that moment, the fog parted. Beth could now see that they were next to a wide river.

Patrick gasped. "Who's that?"

On the river was a man paddling a small boat. The boat was shaped like a round bowl. It was covered with a patchwork of leather.

The man in the boat wore a dark cloak. The cloak's hood was pulled over his face. "You, boy!" the man shouted. "Come and help me dock my boat."

Patrick looked around as if the man had called to someone else.

"I think he means you," Beth whispered.

Patrick frowned and then hurried over to the edge of the river. Beth followed close behind. The heavy fog made her nervous.

The boat drew in closer. Patrick took a step and was suddenly knee-deep in the water. "It's freezing," he said with a groan.

Patrick reached out toward the boat.

The man grabbed Patrick's wrist.

"Hey!" Patrick said. He sounded surprised.

The man pulled Patrick into the boat.

"What are you doing?" Patrick cried out.

Beth rushed forward. She stumbled in the icy water and nearly fell. The man grabbed the neckline of her dress and pulled her into the boat too.

"Two are better than one," the man said. He pushed Beth down to the bottom of the boat. In one fast motion he had a rope in his hands. He quickly tied Patrick's wrists and ankles together.

"Help!" Patrick called out.

Beth struggled to her feet. Another piece of rope seemed to come from nowhere. The man grabbed Beth with strong hands and turned her around.

He instantly bound her wrists and ankles just like Patrick's. "Why are you doing this to us?" Beth asked.

"It's all part of the trade," the man said.

"What trade?" Beth asked.

From beneath his hood he said, "Slaves."

Then the man knelt in the front of the boat with a long oar. He paddled the boat down the river.

Splash . . . splash . . . splash . . .

Beth and Patrick sat in silence. Thick fog made it impossible to see where they were going.

"This isn't the best Saint Patrick's Day I've ever had," Patrick whispered to Beth.

Beth looked up at the man and cleared her throat. "Sir?" she asked. She hoped being polite and showing respect would get him to talk.

The man turned a little. The hood still covered most of his face. Beth saw bits of dried meat stuck to his scruffy beard.

"Where are you taking us?" Beth asked.

"The castle of Tara!" the man said brightly. Then he laughed harshly. "You'll be joining everyone at the great feast."

"The great feast?" Patrick asked.

"Surely you know of it," the man said. "All the grand nobility will be there. Even King Logaire and his beautiful queen."

"I can't wait to meet them," Patrick said.

Beth knew Patrick was being sarcastic.

But the boatman didn't. He said, "It's a grand time. Bards will sing their songs. Teachers will teach their arts. Men will try their skill in chariot races, contests, and games. Everyone in Ireland will be there. Noblemen and common peasants alike."

Ireland, she thought, *that's where Saint Patrick lived.*

"Is the festival even for us lowly slaves?" Beth asked.

"Aye," the man said. "The wise ones will have special tasks for you."

"The wise ones?" Beth asked.

The man lowered his voice to a harsh whisper. "The druids," he said.

Beth shivered. "Patrick," she whispered, "are those the people Mr. Whittaker warned us about?"

The Druids

Patrick nodded to Beth, and then he gulped.
He remembered hearing about druids in
school. The druids weren't very nice.

The boatman paddled harder and faster.
After a few minutes, the boat turned toward
the shore. It slid up on a muddy, flat place at
the river's edge. Then it bumped to a stop.

Two men wearing white, hooded robes
appeared out of the woods. Beth thought
they looked like ghosts in the mist.

One was old. He was short and thin with a long gray beard. The other was big and husky like a bear. His red beard and curly hair stuck out under his white hood.

"Get the slaves, Shane," said the old man with the gray beard.

The big man reached into the boat and grabbed Patrick's arms.

Ugh! Patrick thought. *He stinks worse than I do!*

Shane lifted Patrick out of the boat. He set Patrick down on the muddy shore.

Shane lifted Beth out of the boat too. Then he spoke to the man in the boat. "Where did you find these two?" Shane asked. "They're scrawny."

"Hey!" Beth said. "I'm *slender,* not scrawny."

Shane scowled at her.

"The boy is a swinekeeper," the man whispered. "The girl was with him."

"Swinekeeper!" Patrick said. "I'm not a—"

"Quiet!" Shane said with a snarl. He tossed a pouch into the bottom of the boat.

Clink.

"I expect better-quality slaves next time," Shane said to the hooded man.

The boatman grunted.

Shane untied Patrick. "Push the boat back into the river," he said.

Patrick thought about arguing. He thought about escaping now that he was untied. But Beth was still bound.

Patrick shuffled into the icy water. He pushed on the boat with his shoulder. Hard. It slid into the water.

The man in the boat paddled away. The

boat disappeared into the fog.

Shane grabbed Patrick's arms and tied his wrists again. Then he knelt and did the same to his ankles.

"How are we supposed to walk?" Patrick asked.

"You'll figure it out," Shane said.

Patrick and Beth shuffled forward like a couple of penguins.

Shane and the old man led Patrick and Beth into the nearby woods. The fog gave the trees an eerie look.

"They didn't have monsters in Saint Patrick's time, did they?" Beth whispered.

Patrick looked around. "I hope not," he said nervously.

Then Patrick thought of the druids. He remembered that some monsters were actually human.

The woods opened up to a small clearing. A wooden cart with two oxen was there. In the back of the cart sat several men and women and a girl.

The other people were all dressed in clothes like Patrick's and Beth's. Their hands and feet were tied too. They looked sad and scared.

Patrick thought the girl looked about eight years old. She had curly red hair that fell down past her shoulders.

Shane lifted Patrick into the cart. Then Beth. Next Shane and the old man with the gray beard climbed up to the front of the cart. They sat on a benchlike seat. Shane picked up a whip. He cracked it in the air.

"Hey ya!" Shane shouted at the oxen.

The oxen pulled. The cart moved forward through the mist and into the woods again.

"Move closer to me," Patrick whispered to Beth. "I'll try to untie your hands."

She obeyed. Patrick dug at the rope with his fingers. It was hard, but Patrick loosened the rope. Beth slipped her hands out.

"Now untie my hands," Patrick said to Beth. He kept an eye on Shane and the old man in front. Beth got his hands free. Patrick felt the blood rush back into his hands.

Patrick untied his ankles next. He helped Beth untie her ankles, too.

The other slaves watched them with worried looks.

Patrick whispered to the girl. "I'll untie your ropes," he said.

"Leave my daughter alone, laddie," said the man next to her. His voice was low. "The druids bound her, so bound she will stay."

"Why is everyone afraid of the druids?" Beth asked.

"Do you not know, lassie?" the girl's father asked in surprise. "The druids are the ones who brought us all here. It's theirs to do powerful magic. It's theirs to know the secrets of the gods."

God is the true God, Patrick thought. *There is no other god. The Bible says to stay away from magic. It's evil.*

"They're not here now," Beth said. "So why be afraid?"

"Are you daft? Of course they're here," the girl's father said. "Who do you think is driving the cart?"

Ka-bump!

One of the cart's wheels bounced off a rock. Patrick fell against the side of the cart.

Beth asked him, "What should we do now?"

Patrick didn't have a plan. He watched Shane and the old man. If they were druids, they looked like any other men. Just meaner.

The cart traveled deeper into the woods. Thick fog hung all around them.

"I'm Caera," the red-haired girl whispered to Patrick.

Patrick started to say, "I'm—"

"Stop talking!" Caera's father said in a sharp whisper.

"Why aren't you trying to escape?" Patrick whispered to the other prisoners.

The Fallen Tree

Caera's father frowned. The rest didn't say anything. One woman shook her head and began to cry.

Caera spoke up. "The druids cast spells and put curses on anyone who resists them," she said.

"I don't believe that," Beth said.

Just then the cart rolled out of the woods. A field and then more woods were ahead. The fog was still thick. Suddenly the cart jerked to a stop. A giant oak tree lay across the road. It was impossible to go on.

The old druid with the long gray beard climbed down from the cart. Shane, the big one, followed him. Their flowing robes glowed ghostly white in the mist. They both walked around the fallen tree. The oxen stamped their feet.

Dear God, Patrick prayed. *Please help us!*

A red squirrel climbed up on the edge of the cart. It stared at Patrick, and then it jumped back down again. It scampered across the field toward the woods.

Patrick's eyes followed it. Then he noticed a stranger at the edge of the trees. He looked like a shadow in the fog. Patrick squinted. The figure looked like a young man. The squirrel climbed up his long brown robe and then perched on his shoulder.

"Look," Caera said to the other prisoners. They turned to look. "'Tis Tristan," Caera whispered.

Patrick wondered if Shane and the old man could see the stranger. Patrick could hear the men grunting as they tried to lift the fallen tree. He hoped they weren't paying attention to anything else.

"He's not to be trusted," Caera's father said, frowning. "He's a friend of the bishop."

"The bishop!" Patrick and Beth whispered together. Patrick's heart leaped. Mr. Whittaker had said the bishop would help them.

Beth nudged Patrick and nodded to the stranger. He was motioning for them to come to him in the woods.

"Let's go!" Patrick said. "Tristan wants us to escape!"

Beth slipped down from the back of the cart first. Then Patrick followed.

"Come on!" Patrick whispered to Caera.

"I say not," her father said. "If the druids see us running away, they may use their magic. They'll turn us into beasts."

"They can't do that," Beth said.

Patrick knew that arguing wouldn't help. So he said, "If you stay here, you'll stay enslaved. Or something even more terrible might happen to you."

Caera's father frowned. He looked at his daughter. Then he nodded. "Caera may go with you," he said.

Patrick sighed with relief. He untied Caera's wrists and ankles. Then he helped

Caera climb down.

Suddenly Caera pushed away from Patrick. "No," she said. "I won't go without my father."

Patrick glanced at Caera's father. This was taking far too long. The two druids might come back at any moment.

The father looked at his daughter. He sighed and nodded. Patrick and Beth quickly untied the ropes that bound him. He climbed over the cart's side.

"Hurry!" Beth whispered to the others. But they sat still, frozen in fear.

Tristan motioned to them more urgently.

Patrick kept an eye on the druids. They were still working on the tree. Then he led the other three toward Tristan. Beth tripped and fell over her long dress. Caera helped her back up.

Just then the big druid Shane rounded the cart. "Stop!" he shouted at them.

"Run!" Patrick said to his friends. They dashed into the woods.

They approached Tristan in the woods. He didn't speak to them. Instead, he turned and moved quickly ahead of them. They followed. The squirrel clung to Tristan's shoulder.

Soon they were standing on a strip of moist dirt and rocks. It looked like a dry creek bed. Tristan knelt on the dirt and closed his eyes.

Is he praying? Patrick wondered.

Patrick stepped up to him and knelt down to suggest they hide. Beth crouched next to him. Then Caera and her father joined them.

"This is no place to hide," Caera's father said. "The druids will easily see us."

Tristan seemed to ignore him. Then he lifted his hands. "Lord," Tristan prayed, "may You protect us as You protected the bishop. When the druids tried to capture the bishop and his friends, You showed them Your power. Like deer in the forest, they escaped from danger because of Your help."

There was a loud snapping of branches. Leaves crunched behind them. The big druid was coming!

"Don't move," Tristan said.

"Are you daft?" Caera's father whispered.

"Trust me," Tristan said.

Shane stepped out of the fog a little ways down the creek bed. He stopped and looked straight at them.

6

Escape

Shane stared directly at Beth. She froze as she was and waited for him to point and shout. He looked puzzled. Then he turned away as if he were still searching for them.

The old man shuffled up to Shane. He seemed winded from the run. "Well?" the old man asked. His gaze went to Beth and the others.

"The slaves aren't here," Shane said to the old druid. "I see only those two bucks and their fawns." He nodded toward Beth.

"Shoot them for meat," the old druid said.

"There's no time," Shane said. He stepped away from the creek bed and disappeared. The old druid took one more look in Beth's direction. Then he slowly followed Shane into the fog.

Tristan stood up. The red squirrel made a harsh chattering noise. It sounded as if it were scolding the druids to stay far away.

"Do be quiet, Finn," Tristan said to the squirrel.

The squirrel stopped its chatter.

"Come!" Tristan said to the other three. "They'll keep looking for you."

He led them down the creek bed.

"What just happened?" Beth asked Tristan. "Why didn't they see us?"

"They saw us," Tristan said. "But they didn't see us as we are. God was merciful and allowed them to see something else."

"How is that possible, laddie?" Caera's father asked.

"With God, all things are possible," Tristan said.

"But you're no druid. You're one of the new faith," Caera's father said. "How is it that you do magic?"

Tristan turned to him. "It's not magic," he said. "The power of God is greater than any of the druids' little tricks."

Caera's father looked as if he might say something. But he closed his mouth and looked away.

"Are you a Christian?" Beth asked Tristan.

"I'm a new follower of Christ and a convert

of the bishop," Tristan said.

"Will you take us to the bishop?" Patrick asked.

"I'm on my way to see him now. I stopped because I saw the druids had captured slaves," he said. "You were wise to come with me. I wish the others had the same courage. I know of the druids' terrible plans for you."

"Terrible plans?" asked Beth. "What were they going to do with us?"

"Some of you would have been used as sacrifices," Tristan said.

"Sacrifices!" Patrick cried. "You mean, they would have put us on an altar and—"

"The druids offer sacrifices to their god Cromm Cruaich each year at the festival," Tristan said. "Only the sacrifice of innocent blood is acceptable. Then they believe the people will be granted peaceful lives. But the druids are liars. Their gods can never bring peace. You can find peace only when you believe in the one true God."

For a moment, Tristan seemed radiant. It was as if his words brought out a great light within him.

"Did *you* cause the tree to fall in our path?" Caera asked with a hint of wonder in her voice.

Tristan glanced at her. "It wasn't magic, as you might think," he said. "That tree had been struck by lightning. Its trunk was weak and cracked. So I gave it a mighty shove. It fell onto the trail and blocked the path."

"Thank you," Beth said.

The others agreed.

Tristan smiled at her. "I'm at your service,"

he said.

"But what's to become of us now?" Caera's father asked. "The druids burned our hut. They took our small farm as their own."

"The druids believe everything belongs to them for their own purposes," Tristan said. "I'm sorry for you."

He looked at Patrick and Beth. "And where did they find you?"

"By a riverbank," Beth said.

"With a bunch of pigs," Patrick said.

"Ah, swineherding!" Tristan said. "I have great affection for that skill."

At that moment, they emerged from the woods. The foggy mist was behind them. The sun shone ahead of them. Dark clouds moved onto the nearby mountains.

The dirt path they were on spread out to a

bigger highway. Men riding horses galloped along the wide road. Their clattering hooves kicked up dust. Oxen pulled carts of common folk. Many were dressed in colorful tunics.

"Are they going to celebrate the feast at the castle?" Beth asked.

"Aye," Tristan said. "But they don't know what it is they're celebrating."

Suddenly Beth's eye caught a patch of green on the ground. "Shamrocks!" she said. "Real shamrocks." Beth reached down and picked one. She tucked it into one of the holes on her vest.

Caera smiled. "'Tis pretty to be sure," she said. "I, too, love the shamrock. The clover is a symbol of our beloved land."

"I shall now call you Beth o' the Shamrock," Tristan said.

Beth beamed. She felt as if she'd just been crowned.

The Prophecy

Tristan, the cousins, and the others joined the noisy crowd traveling along the road. Soon they came upon the outskirts of a small village. A group of festive people gathered at the side of the road. A man with a musical instrument stood in the middle of the crowd. The instrument looked like a small harp. The man lifted his head and began to sing.

The man wore a hat in the shape of a

cone. It looked as if it had been made from the bark of a tree. His tunic was a colorful assortment of square patches. His leather shoes pointed up at the toes. As the man sang, he danced a merry jig.

"'Tis our friend Dubbach!" Caera said. "He's a bard."

Beth looked at Patrick. "A bard?" she asked.

"A bard travels from village to village," Caera said. "He cheers us all with his singing and clever wit."

Beth and Patrick drew closer to the bard.

Dubbach the bard finished his song. He stopped dancing. Then he strummed the small harp for a moment. The tune sounded mournful. Then he sang out with a loud clear voice:

A new and bright fire comes.

It burns in the peasants' hearts.

It turns our people from our gods.

Our altars fall apart.

A fire burns in our land.

Oh, who now brings this flame?

Where does he get his powerful light?

Pray, tell me whence he came!

The sad song made Beth feel strange inside. She asked Caera, "What does the song mean?"

"'Tis the prophecy," Caera said.

"What prophecy?" Patrick asked.

Caera's father said, "For ages past, the prophecy has foretold that a fire would come to our land. It would burn away the faith of our fathers. The fire would tear down the altars of our druids. It would change Ireland forever."

"Aye," said Caera. "Some say it could happen soon."

"It's happening *now*," Tristan said. "God has called the bishop to this pagan land. The bishop brings the good news of Jesus Christ."

"But the bishop is not to be trusted," Caera's father said. "He tears down the altars our fathers built. He talks of following new ways."

"The druids built the altars to sacrifice human lives. The killings honor their false gods," Tristan said. "Why is it wrong to end such evil practices? They have hurt our people for generations!"

Tristan paused and stared into the farmer's eyes. "They were going to kill your own child," Tristan said.

Caera's father put a protective arm around his daughter.

Tristan continued. "The bishop does not teach evil. He teaches that hope can be found in Jesus Christ."

By this time, the crowd had turned to Tristan. Some scowled at him. Some clenched their fists.

Finn the squirrel sat up on Tristan's shoulder. The cute animal seemed to calm the crowd. Dubbach stopped his song. He pushed through the crowd to see who had interrupted him. He saw Caera and her father. His face lit up.

The bard stopping singing. Then the crowd drifted away to go about their own business.

"Erc the farmer! Caera!" the bard cried with merriment. "You have come a long way from home for the festival."

"We have no home now," Caera's father, Erc, said sadly. "It was destroyed by fire."

Dubbach frowned and shook his head. "That's a rightful shame," he said.

Suddenly a smile of joy lit up the bard's face. "My cousin Bronus works in the castle at Tara," he said. "He told me yesterday that King Logaire needs skilled workers."

"What would the workers do?" Erc asked.

"They would farm the fields that provide

food for the royal family," Dubbach said.
"Come with me! I'll take you to meet my
cousin. He'll find work and a new home for
you at the castle."

Caera's father bowed to Dubbach the
bard. Then he turned and bowed to Tristan.
"I will repay you one day for your great
kindness," he said.

Tristan nodded with a smile. "God is
watching over you," he said.

Erc turned to Caera and said, "Come,
lassie." He joined Dubbach, and the two
men walked away.

Caera looked up at Tristan. "I would like
to know more about the bishop and the new
ways," she said.

Tristan nodded and said, "I'll see to it."

Caera waved good-bye to Beth and Patrick.

She raced after her father.

"This is a strange place," Beth said to Patrick. "The people don't know about God."

Patrick opened his mouth to reply, but suddenly he stopped. He looked beyond Beth, and his eyes grew wide.

Beth spun around. A cart pulled by two oxen headed straight toward them. Shane and the old druid were driving it. Over a dozen people sat tied up in the back. A soldier on horseback galloped beside the cart.

"There they are!" shouted Shane to the soldier. "It's one of the bishop's converts. And our slaves. They're leading a rebellion against the high king! Catch them!"

8

Finn

The soldier galloped toward them. He
held his shield against his side. His sword
glimmered in the sun.

Then several things happened at once.

"Follow me!" Tristan shouted to the
cousins. He turned to run into the crowd.
Finn jumped off Tristan's shoulder. He
scampered into a forest of legs and feet.
Patrick tugged at Beth's arm and took off
after Tristan.

Beth couldn't take her eyes off the soldier. She stood frozen in fear. She heard Patrick call from somewhere behind her.

The soldier's horse galloped up to Beth. The soldier reached out his hand for her.

"Beth!" Patrick cried out.

Beth's feet felt as if they suddenly grew wings. She ducked the soldier's grasp and scrambled toward the crowd. She ran past Patrick, and he followed close behind her.

Beth pushed through the confused crowd. A pig stepped in her way. She dodged it. Then she bowled into a flock of sheep. They scattered. She slid under a cart filled with fish. Then she rolled out the other side.

Patrick stayed with her every step of the way.

Beth ran into another crowd. The village's

crowds, animals, and carts kept the soldier from following. His shouts sounded farther and farther away.

Beth saw Finn up ahead and wondered where Tristan had gone. Finn darted behind a hut. Beth and Patrick followed him.

They reached a grassy field. The sky above was dark with clouds. Finn reached the edge of a wooded hill. He climbed up a tall tree. Then he raced from branch to branch. He jumped and leaped deeper into the woods.

Beth and Patrick followed Finn from the ground. The hill got steeper and steeper. It was hard to keep up.

A light rain sprinkled down and soaked Beth's clothes and skin. Then the sky opened up and a heavy, cold rain washed over her. She looked at Patrick. He was drenched too.

Patrick grabbed Beth's sleeve. "Let's head that way," he said. He pointed to a wall of rock. "I see some caves. We can find shelter there."

The cousins ran to the rock wall. They crawled underneath a large rock ledge. They sat for a moment, gasping.

Beth looked out through the rain to make sure the soldier wasn't following them. She could see beyond the trees to the valley below. Across the valley stood a castle on another hill.

"That's probably the castle Tara," Beth said. She was still a little breathless.

"It looks spooky," Patrick said. "I wonder if anyone is locked up in the pointy tower."

"Probably kids who didn't obey the druids," Beth said.

Finn suddenly appeared between them. He shook his fur and licked his paws.

"Where is Tristan?" Beth asked Finn.

He shook his head from side to side.

"He's a squirrel," Patrick said as if to suggest that she was silly to talk to it.

"Dogs seem to know what we're saying," Beth said. "Maybe Tristan has Finn trained."

Patrick looked doubtful.

The cousins rested while the storm passed. Finally the rain stopped. But a chilly wind whipped around the hill. The sun was setting. Finn suddenly chattered and ran off again.

"I think it's time to go," Beth said.

The cousins followed Finn. The red squirrel

stopped at the edge of a clearing and climbed a large tree.

Beth and Patrick hid behind the tree and peered ahead.

A group of thirty men moved around the top of the hill. They were throwing branches into a big pile. The men's long brown robes were muddy and wet.

A tall, bald man with a cropped white beard stood in the middle of them. He seemed to be giving instructions to the others. He was holding a tall staff. It reminded Beth of the staff she had seen in pictures of Jesus as the Good Shepherd.

Beth's heart pounded in her ears. *What are they going to do with all that wood?* she wondered. *Is this a secret meeting of the druids?*

The Bishop

Beth looked up at Finn in the tree above her. He sat on a branch, eating a pinecone.

Just then Tristan walked into the clearing from a different part of the forest.

Ka-thunk. Finn dropped his pinecone. It nearly hit Patrick on the head. Finn raced down the tree trunk to the ground. Then he scampered across the clearing, climbed up Tristan's robe, and sat on his shoulder.

"Finn!" Tristan said in surprise. "Where

have you been? And where are the others?"

"Here we are!" Beth cried. She stepped out into the clearing. Patrick stepped out with her.

Tristan smiled. "I'm so glad you're all right," he said. "I lost you in the village."

"Finn led us here," Beth said.

Tristan looked at Finn. "Well done," he said to the squirrel.

The tall man turned his attention to Tristan. "Tristan!" He came down the hill and clasped the young man by both arms. "I'm pleased you've arrived."

Tristan gave a respectful bow of his head. "I am too," he said. "I wondered if I would make it safely. God protected us in miraculous ways."

The man turned to Beth and Patrick. "Who

are your young friends?" he asked Tristan. Beth noticed that the new man's accent was different from the ones she had heard so far. She wondered if he was from another part of Ireland.

"These children were captured as slaves," Tristan said. "This is Patrick the Keeper of Swine and Beth o' the Shamrock. They were on Shane's cart."

"But Tristan rescued us," Beth said.

"Thanks be to God," said the man. "I'm Patricius, son of Calpornius."

Tristan leaned down and said in a loud whisper, "This is the bishop."

Beth was relieved. She felt as if nothing bad could happen to them now.

"You are both Christians?" the bishop asked.

"Yes," Beth and Patrick said together.

The bishop smiled gently. "You're welcome here to celebrate Christ with us."

Beth noticed markings sewn into his clothes. They were shaped like a cross.

Patrick asked, "Why are you building a huge pile of sticks?"

The bishop looked at the stack of wood. "We're going to light the paschal fire here on Slane Hill," he said.

Beth didn't know what a paschal fire was. And she wondered why Slane Hill was the place to light it.

"Is the fire important?" Beth asked.

The bishop and Tristan looked at each other.

"There is an ancient law. It declares that only the king can light a paschal fire—an Easter fire—on this night," Tristan said. "It's a law made up by the druids, who want to honor their terrible gods tonight."

"So you're breaking the law?" Beth asked. "Won't that get you in trouble?"

The bishop nodded. "Anyone else who lights a fire tonight faces immediate death," he said.

"Death!" Patrick said. "Then why would you do it?"

"It's the best way to challenge the gods of the druids," the bishop said. "The people will be gathered for the festival. They will all see for themselves that the true King is Jesus Christ."

Tristan pointed across the valley to the castle. "That is the castle of Tara," he said. "All the druids are gathering there in King Logaire's courts tonight. They will see our fire and come."

The bishop said in a strong voice, "It will be like Elijah when he challenged the prophets of Baal. We will light a paschal fire. We will battle against the druids' evil black magic."

"But if the druids catch you," Beth said, "they'll kill you."

The bishop smiled gently at Beth. "I'm not afraid of death," he said. "I was once a slave in this pagan land. Irish pirates kidnapped me from my native home in England. They brought me here."

The bishop pointed at Patrick. "I was the slave of one of the druids," the bishop said. "I wore the garb of a swinekeeper. As you wear one now."

Patrick looked down at his clothes.

The bishop continued, "I faced hardship, struggle, and toil every day. It almost destroyed my body."

"That must have been terrible!" Beth said.

"Terrible for my body," the bishop said, "but glorious for my soul. During those hard days I gave my heart to Jesus. I stared into the face of death many times. But I also looked into the face of Jesus. To die here on this earth is to stand in His presence."

The bishop's followers had stopped their work to listen. Then one shouted, "We are not afraid of death!" Others joined in. Then came another shout: "Light the fire!"

The bishop moved back to the pile of branches. One of the men gave the bishop a thick stick covered with black tar.

Tristan stepped over to the cousins. He

petted Finn's head. "Stay with Patrick," he said to the squirrel. "I don't want you too near the fire."

Finn leaped from Tristan's shoulder to Patrick's. Patrick looked uneasy. He nodded at Tristan.

"I suggest you move farther away to watch," Tristan said. Then he turned and joined the bishop and his men.

Beth and Patrick and Finn moved down the hill. Beth stood close to Patrick. Finn chattered and barked.

The hillside fell into shadow. The darkness made her afraid. She expected the druids and the soldiers to spring from the woods. Then she realized that they might arrest her too.

Am I afraid of death? she wondered.

The Challenge

Patrick and Beth watched the men stack the final pieces of wood. The tower of sticks stood taller than the bishop.

Some of the men crouched down. They seemed busy with something near the ground. Then one of the men threw a stone away in frustration. Another growled and kicked a piece of wood.

"Why are they upset?" Beth asked.

"They can't get the fire started," Patrick

said. "It's too windy. And the wood is probably wet from that rain."

"Then how will they challenge the druids?" Beth asked.

Just then Patrick remembered the gift Whit had given him. "My tinderbox!" Patrick said to Beth. "Hurry! Let's find some dry twigs and leaves."

Patrick and Beth ran back to the woods. Finn jumped from Patrick's shoulder as if he might help them. The cousins looked underneath thick trees for dry wood. They picked up a few pieces. They also found dry bark strips and grass underneath.

They took everything they had gathered back to the top of the hill. The bishop's men were busy trying to start the fire by striking rocks. Sparks flew, but the wood wouldn't catch fire.

"We're losing time!" Tristan cried.

"God will provide," the bishop said. "Search the forest for drier wood and better rocks to start the fire."

"Should I tell them?" Beth asked Patrick.

"Not until I'm sure this will work," Patrick said.

Patrick knelt down and made a small pile out of the bark and grass.

"Sit on that side," Patrick said to Beth. "That will help block the wind."

Beth crouched near the pile.

Patrick opened the tinderbox. He held the flint rock in one hand. He held the bar of steel in the other.

Patrick struck the flint and steel together several times. Sparks flew. One tiny spark landed on the little piece of cloth in the tinderbox. The cloth caught fire.

Patrick used the burning cloth to light the little pile of bark and grass. The fire grew.

The light caught the bishop's attention. He was suddenly at their side. The big man knelt down next to Patrick. Then he clapped his hands.

"It's working," Patrick said, relieved.

"It is fitting that children—innocents— have helped in this glorious event," the bishop said. "Now stand back."

Beth and Patrick stood and backed away from the small fire.

Patricius placed the torch in the flame for

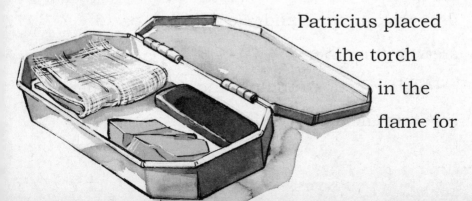

several seconds. Suddenly the pitch on the outside of the torch flamed to life.

Finn crawled up Patrick's arm to his shoulder. He made more barking noises.

The bishop raised the torch in the air. "The druids have led this people into a dark age. We will show them that the light of Jesus is more powerful than their magic!"

The bishop went to the base of the pile. "Tonight," the bishop shouted, "let it be known in all the land that Patricius, bishop of Ireland, lit the paschal fire!"

The bishop threw the torch onto the huge pile of wood.

Soon the whole pile was ablaze with a roaring fire. Huge orange and red flames leaped up high in the night sky.

Patrick and Beth moved back from the

bright flame. The fire rose upward to the sky. The flames looked as if they might light the dim stars.

"I'll bet all of Ireland can see that," Patrick said.

The bishop stood in front of the roaring flames. He looked toward the hill of Tara. A crowd of druids gathered outside the castle walls. The bishop threw his arms open wide. "Lochru, evil lord of the druids! Hear now the words I say. Tonight I challenge you and your dark faith."

A great cheer rose up from the bishop's followers. An angry roar echoed from the druids on the hill of Tara.

Beth looked and gasped. She grabbed Patrick's arm. "Look! They're coming!" she cried. "The druids have lit fires now too."

Patrick turned toward the castle. The druids' torches were moving in their direction in a wave of flames.

At that moment, Tristan came to the cousins' side. "I would send you somewhere safe, but I don't know that such a place exists."

Finn jumped down from Patrick's shoulder. Then the red squirrel climbed up Tristan's brown robe. He perched again on Tristan's shoulder.

Tristan squinted in the direction of Tara. He said, "I see a great cloud of white-robed figures moving down the hillside. Lord Lochru, the chief of all the druids, leads the way."

They could see one large man at the head of the crowd.

Tristan said softly, "He holds our nation captive with sorcery."

"Why do the people let Lochru get away with it?" Patrick asked.

"Lochru is a friend of King Logaire, the most important king in Ireland," said Tristan. "Lochru whispers his prophecies and threats in the king's ear. King Logaire is afraid. So he obeys Lochru's commands."

They watched as the druids disappeared from view.

"They'll be climbing Slane Hill soon," Tristan said.

"Are you afraid?" Beth asked, sounding very afraid.

"The bishop taught me not to fear the things that can kill the body," Tristan said.

"How did the bishop become so powerful?"

Patrick asked. "He said he was a slave and a swinekeeper."

"The bishop escaped from slavery here in Ireland," Tristan said. "He sailed back to his home in England. But he saw visions from God. In the visions, God called him to come back to this dark land and shine the light of Christ. Patricius was ordained by the church and sent here as a bishop."

Patrick heard loud shouts coming from the woods. Torches flickered among the trees. The small flames grew brighter. Men in white hoods and robes arrived at the clearing.

Patrick reached over to Beth and drew her behind him.

One druid stepped forward. His long white beard flowed down to his waist. He lifted his druid's staff high in the air. "I am Lochru," he shouted. "I demand to know who lit this fire! Come forth and tell us your name if you dare!"

Patrick looked at the tinderbox in his hand. He felt a surge of anger flow through him. Maybe it was courage. He didn't like the druids. He didn't like how they hurt the people with their lies. Suddenly he wanted Lochru to know that he had lit the fire.

"I did," Patrick said. His voice sounded nervous to his own ears. "And my name is Patrick."

Lord Lochru

Patrick felt a hand fall on his shoulder an instant later.

"I am responsible for this fire," the bishop said from behind Patrick. His tone was warm. But there was a lion's strength behind it. "I am Patricius, bishop of Christ's church."

Lochru waved a bony finger at the bishop. "How dare you challenge the ancient laws of our land!" he cried.

The fire crackled and roared behind them. Branches crashed down. A spray of hot sparks flew high into the air.

Lochru pointed his staff toward the fire. "Put out this fire at once!" he shouted.

The druids moved toward the flames. Some grabbed dirt and threw it onto the fire. Others tossed large clumps of wet leaves. But the fire burned hotter.

"We need water!" one druid called out.

"Bring water from the creek!" Lochru shouted.

A few of the druids hurried to obey.

Lochru turned to the remaining druids. "Guard those two," he said. "The king will see that they're punished!"

The druids moved toward the bishop and Patrick.

"Take the girl away," the bishop said quietly to Tristan.

Beth looked surprised. Tristan raised his hand as if he might protest.

"*Now*," the bishop ordered.

Tristan nodded. Then he grabbed Beth's arm and began to pull her toward the woods.

Beth dragged her feet. "No," she said. "I want to stay with Patrick."

"Go with Tristan," Patrick said. "We'll be safe."

Suddenly Lochru laughed loudly. "Safe?" he shouted. "You will be *dead*!"

● ● ●

Tristan and Beth hid in the forest. They silently watched the clearing from behind some bushes. The light from the fire shone around the crowd for hundreds of feet.

Hour after hour the druids brought buckets of water up the hill. They threw the water on the flames, but the fire stayed lit. Then more druids came with more water buckets. But the fire only burned brighter as each bucket was emptied on the flames.

Beth was about to fall asleep against a tree. But she heard a strange sound.

Rumble! Rumble! Rumble!

The ground shook.

Rumble! Rumble! Rumble!

"What's that noise?" Beth whispered to Tristan. "It sounds like an earthquake."

"Look and see," Tristan said. He pointed to the clearing.

Beth and Tristan watched the chariots arrive. They were pulled by galloping horses.

Soldiers rode in the chariots. Each carried a shield in one hand and had a sword at his side. They headed straight toward the druids.

The chariots stopped. A soldier stepped out from one of the chariots. "We come with orders from the high king," he said to the group of druids.

Lochru stepped up to meet them. "Speak!" he cried.

"King Logaire summons the one who lit this fire to appear before him," the soldier said. "He will be charged with a sentence of death."

The bishop rose to his feet. "I will gladly come," he said. "Thanks be to God! This is the reason I built the fire."

"What about the boy?" Lochru asked. "He

admitted that he helped!"

"What do I care about a boy?" the soldier asked.

Just then a big druid with red hair stepped out of the crowd of white robes.

Beth gasped. It was Shane.

"*I* care!" Shane shouted. "The boy is an escaped slave! I paid a bagful of gold for him."

Lochru turned. He pounded his staff on the ground. "Bring him along! To the castle!" he cried.

"Walk behind us!" shouted the soldier. He climbed back into his chariot. He gave a command. All the chariots turned. The horses galloped away. They pulled the chariots back toward the castle.

The bishop and Patrick marched after the soldiers. The men in brown robes fell in line behind the bishop.

Bong. Bong. Bong.

A solemn drum sounded. One of the bishop's followers pounded a steady beat as they walked.

Beth thought the drum sounded like a death march.

Princesses

Beth wrung her hands in worry.

"Don't be afraid, Beth o' the Shamrock," Tristan said. "We'll ask God to deliver our friends."

Tristan moved away from the rising sun and the fire. He walked into the dark woods. "Follow me," he said.

Beth obeyed. Tristan picked up his pace as they walked down the hill.

They reached the valley. Then Tristan

followed a path up the hill to Tara. They came up behind the castle. Its tall gray walls looked like ancient stones piled up to the sky.

Tristan pushed hard on a small, heavy wooden door.

The door opened up into a little garden. A high hedge surrounded it. Orange and red flowers waved at them in the morning sunshine.

Beth noticed a small girl kneeling in the middle of the garden. The girl was placing food and pretty plates on a purple carpet. It looked as if she was preparing a picnic.

The girl wore a pretty yellow dress. Her hair was bright red and curly.

The girl turned toward Beth and Tristan. It was Caera.

Caera looked surprised. "'Tis Beth o' the Shamrock! And Tristan!" she said. "What are you doing here?"

Tristan laughed. "I might ask you the same thing," he said. "Only yesterday you wore the clothes of a farmer's daughter. Now look at you!"

Caera smiled again. She said, "Dubbach found my father a job here. He tends the king's farms. The queen made me a lady-in-waiting. Today I'm preparing breakfast for the royal daughters."

Tristan turned to Beth. "Perhaps the Lord of heaven has planned it," he said. "Stay here with Caera while I make sure we're safe."

Tristan gave a half-bow to the girls. Then he hurried off with Finn following him.

Caera asked, "What did he mean by 'safe'? Are you in trouble?"

Beth nodded. But before she could tell Caera what had happened, Beth heard quick footsteps. They were coming from the other side of the high garden hedge.

Then she saw two pretty girls run through an opening in the hedge. They stood next to Caera. They looked a little older than Beth. They were dressed in long dresses. The dress fabric was woven from golden thread and covered with tiny jewels.

"Caera, who is this?" asked the girl with blonde hair.

"What is she doing here?" asked the girl with red hair.

Caera curtsied to the girls. "Princess Ethne the Fair, meet Beth o' the Shamrock,"

Caera said. "And Princess Fedelm the Red, also meet my friend. Beth is a friend of the bishop too."

Both princesses clapped their hands. "Tell us about the bishop!" they cried. "We've heard about him and his new God."

Caera knelt down and cleared a space on the carpet. She helped the princesses sit down. Beth sat down also. Then Caera stood next to them.

Beth didn't know how to begin teaching about God. Then she remembered the shamrock in her vest. It gave her an idea.

She showed them the shamrock. "There is one true God," she said. She pointed to one of the three leaves. "There is God the Father," she said.

Beth pointed to a second green leaf.

"There is God the Son," she said. "His name is Jesus." Beth pointed to the third green leaf and said, "There is God the Holy Spirit. The three are one God. Just as these three leaves are one shamrock."

"Where does this God live?" Fedelm the Red asked. "Is He in the heavens or somewhere on earth?"

Beth thought a minute. Then she said, "God is the Creator of everything. He is high King over the heavens and the earth!"

Caera pointed to the third leaf.

"Tell us about this other one. The Holy Spirit," she said carefully.

"God sent the Holy Spirit to teach us how to love one another," Beth said.

Caera's face shone with joy. "'Tis wondrous to think about," she said. "A God of love who created every beautiful thing."

"That it is," Ethne the Fair said. "This God sounds so different from the gods of the druids. Does this God demand that people be sacrificed?"

Beth shook her head. She touched the second leaf. "Jesus sacrificed Himself for the whole world," she said. "Nobody else needs to die."

Then Ethne the Fair asked, "Is this what the bishop teaches?"

Beth nodded. "Yes. He wants to spread the love of Jesus to your people."

The girls looked wide-eyed.

"I think a God of love is far better than the druid gods," Ethne said.

"If you believe what I told you about Jesus," Beth said, "you can become a Christian."

Caera said, "I believe it."

Fedelm frowned. She said, "It's dangerous to defy the druids."

Beth suddenly remembered Patrick and stood up. "I know," she said. "The druids took my cousin to meet the king. He may be killed for lighting the paschal fire last night."

She began to panic. Tristan had told her to wait there to be safe. But she didn't care about her own safety anymore. "Do you know where they are?" she asked.

Poison

The princesses explained the fastest way to the great hall. Beth first had to find the kitchen. Then she had to follow the servants to the great banquet room.

"You must hurry!" Ethne said. "My father is a fair man. But Lochru is powerful."

"But what can a girl do?" Caera asked.

"I don't know," Beth said. "God will tell me what to do."

Beth thanked the princesses and curtsied.

Then she started running and cut through the hedge. She was worried that Patrick could be sacrificed. *There must be something I can do to help!* she thought.

Inside the castle walls was a tiny village. Beth was glad that the princesses had given her directions. Even so, she had to look inside several buildings. At last she found the kitchen.

Shiny pots and pans hung from hooks on the walls. Great tables overflowed with foods of every kind. Stacks of golden dishes and goblets were off to the side.

A movement caught Beth's eye. A man stood alone at a side table. He was pouring drinks from a jug into three golden chalices. Beth thought he was a servant. She almost stepped forward to ask him where the great hall was. Then she recognized the man.

It was *Lochru*!

What is he doing in the kitchen? she wondered. She crouched down out of view behind a table and watched.

Lochru finished filling the chalices. Then he reached in a pocket in his white robe. He pulled out a small silver flask. He dripped a few drops from the flask into one of the chalices. Then he returned the flask to his pocket.

He glanced around as he put the three chalices on a gold tray. Then he picked up the tray, turned, and walked out.

 Beth suspected that Lochru had put

something bad in one of the chalices. *But what? she wondered. Poison? A sleeping potion?*

She carefully moved out from behind the table. She began to follow Lochru. He would lead her to the banquet room.

Lochru moved down the hallway with the tray.

How can I warn them about the drink? Beth wondered.

She stepped into the hallway and looked around. Tapestries hung along the long wall. She moved near them. She thought she could duck behind one if anyone came. Suddenly she heard a soft brushing noise above her. She looked up. A red squirrel sat on the rod holding one of the tapestries.

"Finn!" she whispered.

The squirrel stopped and looked down at her.

Beth looked quickly at Lochru. He was at the far end of the hallway. He stopped for a moment to adjust the tray. Then he stepped through a high doorway to what looked like a flight of stone steps.

Just then a heavy hand grabbed Beth's shoulder from behind.

● ● ●

Shane pushed Patrick into the magnificent banquet room. The great hall was crowded, and so Shane and Patrick had to stand in the back. Shane kept a grip on Patrick's arm, so Patrick couldn't slip away.

But Patrick could still see everything.

King Logaire sat at the head of the royal banquet table. The beautiful queen sat next to him. They both wore small crowns of gold on their heads. The king wore a rich cape over his tunic made of soft brown fur. The cape was clasped at his right shoulder with a golden brooch.

The queen's dress was a pale, shimmering blue. Over her shoulders she wore a long flowing cape. She wore gold bracelets on her wrists and ankles. Her golden-red hair reached almost to the floor.

Soldiers stood guard behind them.

The bishop was standing tall in the center of the room. His band of followers stood against the right side wall. Tristan stood among them. A crowd of druids in white robes sat in a balcony above the bishop.

Men and women in colorful clothes were seated at tables around the room. Standing along the walls were other people wearing the clothes of common laborers.

They were all waiting for something.

Then Lochru came through a side door carrying a tray with drinks. He went to the king's table and set the tray down. He spoke quietly to the king. The king listened and then responded. Patrick couldn't hear what they were saying. Once or twice Lochru gestured toward the bishop.

The king frowned.

This isn't good for the bishop, Patrick thought.

● ● ●

Beth was staring into the face of a red-cheeked servant woman.

"Beggar," the woman said with a spray of spit. "You'll not get a bite of the king's food.

Go away!" She pushed Beth away from the banquet room.

Beth tried to dodge her. "You don't understand," she said.

The woman grabbed Beth by the skirt. Beth pulled away. Her pocket ripped open, and the acorns inside rolled to the ground.

Suddenly a ball of red fur flew through the air. Finn had jumped from the tapestry rod to the floor. He pounced on the acorns.

The squirrel startled the servant woman. She let go of Beth.

"Get out of here you dirty rodent!" the woman shouted at Finn. The she chased Finn down the hallway away from the banquet room.

Beth saw her chance. She rushed up the

stairs and into the banquet room.

She thought, *The acorns have been used. Someone is in great danger—I must act quickly!*

The High King

The first thing Beth saw was Lochru. He stood in the great banquet hall right in front of the king and queen. He was holding his staff. The three golden chalices were on the table next to him. A small loaf of bread sat on the table too.

The bishop stood next to Lochru.

Beth scanned the room for Patrick. She saw him near a back wall next to Shane.

Beth began to move along the side of the

room. She wanted to reach the chalices.

Lochru stepped forward. He pointed his staff at the bishop. "This traitor lit a fire on the day none may be lit," he said. "The king knows that the penalty is death!"

"It is an ancient druid law," the bishop said calmly. He looked at Lochru. "It is a law meant to bring death, as all of their laws do."

"My king—" Lochru began to say.

The king held up his hand for silence.

Lochru bowed slightly and kept quiet.

The king said to the bishop, "You lit the fire in defiance of the druids. You are willing to die for this God of yours. Why?"

"Because He brings peace and truth to your people," the bishop said. "His truth is not like the lies and death that the druids bring."

"Words," Lochru said. "Mere words."

"I am trying to understand," said the king. "Show me the power of your God."

"I will not attempt to impress you with tricks," the bishop said. "You must believe by faith."

Then Lochru said to the bishop, "Do you have a custom of eating bread and drinking together?"

"It is true," said the bishop.

Lochru ignored him and quickly turned to the king. "Your Highness," he said. "Let us drink and eat with this Christian according to their custom. You will see whether it has power or not. Then Your Highness will know the truth."

Beth knew this was the moment Lochru had been waiting for.

The king nodded in agreement. "So be it. I

want to experience this custom for myself."

"Look," Lochru said. "I have here on this table our bread and our drinks."

"Your Highness," the bishop said, "it will not work as Lochru suggests."

 The king shook his head. "Let us proceed," he said.

It's now or never, Beth thought. *I've got to act.*

Beth stepped forward to the center of the hall. She curtsied to Lochru. "I am your servant," she said. "I will serve the drinks."

Lochru looked puzzled. But he handed Beth one of the chalices. "Serve this to King Logaire," he said.

Beth carried the chalice to the king. She handed it to him. Then she curtsied and returned to Lochru.

The druid handed Beth a second chalice. "Serve this to the Christian," he said.

Beth carried the chalice to the bishop. She handed it to him. "It's poisoned," she whispered. She curtsied and made her way back to the wall.

Lochru pounded his staff. He held up his chalice. "Let us drink together," he said.

"Wait!" the bishop said. "Our custom of eating bread and drinking together is not a simple one. It has deep meaning for us. It shows our love and unity of faith. So we *share* a chalice."

"Share?" Lochru asked.

The bishop raised the chalice Beth had

given him. "I pray over my chalice and then pass it on for others to drink. So you must drink from *this* chalice, Lochru," he said. He held the chalice out.

Lochru narrowed his eyes. "That seems foolish," he said.

"You said you wanted to honor our custom," the bishop said.

Lochru turned pale. He didn't seem to know what to say.

The bishop smiled at him. "Or if you will not take it, I may pass the chalice to the king," he said.

The bishop handed his chalice to King Logaire. Lochru looked frozen with fear.

"That's the way we share the cup," the bishop said.

"It seems rather simple," the king said

and raised his chalice to his lips. "I will be interested to see what it does to me."

Beth watched the bishop. *Surely he will stop this,* she thought. But he didn't move. Patricius's eyes were closed as if he was praying. He looked calm and at peace.

Beth closed her eyes and prayed too. *Please, God, stop the druids from hurting anyone.*

When she opened her eyes, the chalice was very near the king's lips.

Then Lochru shouted, "Stop!"

The king lowered his chalice.

"What is it, Lochru?" asked King Logaire.

"You must not drink that," Lochru said.

"Why not?" the king asked.

"Because . . . because . . ." Lochru seemed lost for words.

The bishop stepped forward and said, "You must not drink it because Lochru has poisoned it."

King Logaire dropped his chalice on the floor. "Poisoned!"

Lochru looked shaken. He pointed to the bishop and said, "He knows because *he* poisoned it!"

The king stood up. Anger flashed in his eyes. "How? When?" he shouted at Lochru. "*You* brought in the chalices!"

Lochru bowed slightly, his head hung down. "Your Highness," he said. "I didn't mean any harm. I meant for *him* to drink it. To give him the death he deserved."

"Out!" shouted King Logaire. "You and all your druids are to leave immediately!"

"But Your Highness!" Lochru cried.

"Out, I command you!" King Logaire said. "If your laws are just, then you wouldn't have resorted to poison to get justice!"

Lochru took a few steps away. "My king—"

"How often have you done such things to my people?" the king asked.

Lochru shook his head. "What I have done, I have done for you," he said.

The king's eyes narrowed. "Not for me," he said. "You have done it for your own power. Why have I not seen it until now? You have made us slaves to your darkness and fear for too long."

Lochru raised his hands, pleading.

"From this day forth, you and your druids are banished from our land," the king shouted for all to hear. "This is my command! Guards!"

Soldiers rushed forward, their swords ready. They took Lochru by the arms and led him out of the banquet hall. The other druids in the balcony left too.

Shane clamped his hand down on Patrick's shoulder. The druid began to drag Patrick with him.

"Wait, Your Highness," the bishop called out. "There is one among us who is also a victim of the druids. This one is now threatened with slavery."

"Who?" the king asked. "Show him to me."

The bishop pointed to Patrick and Shane. "A mere swinekeeper who was stolen by that enslaver," the bishop said.

"Release him!" the king said to Shane. "Set him free."

Shane took his hand off Patrick's shoulder.

CHALLENGE ON THE HILL OF FIRE

Beth rushed toward her cousin. Tristan also moved to Patrick's side.

Shane followed the remaining druids out of the hall.

King Logaire looked at the bishop. "Now, Christian," he said, "tell us more about this Jesus in whom you trust. I want to know more about this peace He promises."

"Thanks be to God!" the bishop said.

Then he began to speak.

● ● ●

Tristan led Patrick and Beth through a side door and out of the hall. They followed a small corridor to narrow steps. They walked down to another door and stepped out into the sunshine.

"So, you're free," Tristan said. "Will you go home, or would you like to stay with us?"

From somewhere nearby, Beth heard a familiar humming sound. She saw the Imagination Station sitting near a well.

Beth looked at Patrick. He had seen it too.

"Home," Patrick said.

Beth nodded. "It's time to go," she said.

Patrick smiled and said, "We have to tell our people about following the one true God."

"And you, Beth o' the Shamrock?" Tristan asked.

Beth smiled. "I'll use a shamrock to explain about God," she said.

"Go with my blessings," Tristan said. He glanced back toward the great hall. "I must return to the bishop."

As usual, Finn seemed to appear from nowhere. The squirrel climbed up Tristan's robe to his shoulder. "Just in time to say good-bye," Tristan said.

Beth reached up and shook Finn's paw. He chattered with excitement.

"Good-bye!" Beth and Patrick called out together. They walked toward the Imagination Station.

"Good-bye," Tristan said. He turned and headed back inside the banquet hall.

The cousins climbed inside the machine. The door slid closed. *Swoosh!*

Beth pushed the red button.

The Workshop

Patrick and Beth burst out of the Imagination Station and into the workshop. They were wearing the same clothes they wore before their adventure.

Mr. Whittaker looked up from his workbench. "Well? Did you find a pot of gold?" he asked.

"What?" Patrick asked. Then he remembered Jake's plans to build a leprechaun trap.

"We saw some gold," Beth said. "The king wore a gold brooch. The queen had gold jewelry. And the princesses even had gold sewn into their dresses. But there weren't any rainbows with gold at the end."

"No," Whit said. "Like believing in leprechauns, some legends are just wishful thinking."

Beth nodded. But Patrick was quiet.

"What are you thinking about?" Whit asked him.

Patrick frowned. "What a terrible time that was to live," he said. "Sacrifices and slavery . . . Everyone was sad, scared, or angry. Even the ones with money and power."

Beth nodded. She said, "Except the bishop's men. They didn't seem to care about any of that. They only wanted people to know the truth."

Whit smiled at the cousins. "The Christians found the *real* treasure," he said.

Patrick's eyes lit up. "That's what you meant when you said we'd find treasure more valuable than gold," he said.

"That's right," Whit said. "For a while, the people of Ireland understood that too—thanks to Bishop Patricius."

"That wasn't his real name, was it?" Patrick said.

"That's his real name in Latin," Whit said. "In English, it's—"

"Patrick," Beth said.

Whit chuckled. "So you see," he said to Patrick, "you have someone very important who shares your name. Maybe you saw things in him that you'd like to imitate?"

Patrick nodded. "I'd like to stand up to guys like Lochru who bully people with their lies and pain."

"That's a noble idea," Whit said. "Bishop Patrick spent the rest of his life teaching people in Ireland about Jesus. After Bishop Patrick lit the paschal fire and met the druids in the banquet hall, it was the end of the druid religion in

Ireland."

"So the king kept his word," Beth said.

Whit said, "More than that, King Logaire gave Bishop Patrick permission to share the gospel freely all throughout the land. Thousands of Irish men, women, and children gave up their old ways. People from all walks of life became Christians. Rich and poor. Slave and free. After that, missionaries

were sent out from Ireland and spread the gospel across the rest of Europe. In some ways, it started with Patrick."

"Then I guess it can start with us, too," Patrick said. "Maybe I'll talk to Jake and his friends. I can tell them the *real* reason to celebrate Saint Patrick's Day."

"And I'll use my shamrock pin to tell them about God," Beth said.

"That's a good idea," Whit said. Then he looked at them over his glasses. "You know, there are a lot of other Christians who changed history too."

The cousins looked at each other and smiled.

"Come back tomorrow," Whit said. "The Imagination Station will be waiting for you!"

Questions about Bishop Patrick

Q: Why are shamrocks a symbol for Saint Patrick's Day?

A: Legends say that Bishop Patrick used the three-leaf clover to teach the Irish people about the Trinity. The Trinity is made up of God the Father, Jesus the Son, and the Holy Spirit. (See chapter 12.)

Q: Why is green the color of Saint Patrick's Day? Did Bishop Patrick wear green robes?

A: Green represents Ireland. Green is one of the three colors in Ireland's flag. Ireland is also called the Emerald Isle because of its green hills. However, Bishop Patrick wore light-blue robes.

For more info on Bishop Patrick and Ireland, visit *TheImaginationStation.com*.

Secret Word Puzzle

One day King Logaire's daughters, Ethne and Fedelm, went to a lake with a fountain. They found Bishop Patrick and his followers camping nearby. After talking to the bishop, the two princesses became Christians. Ethne and Fedelm were baptized in the fountain that day.

To discover the name of the fountain, find the correct path on the maze. Next write the letters you passed through in the boxes below the maze. The letters will spell the name of the fountain, which is also the secret word.

1	2	3	4	5	6	7

Go to **TheImaginationStation.com**
Find the cover of this book. Click on
"Secret Word." Type in the correct answer,
and you'll receive a prize.

FOCUS ON THE FAMILY® PRESENTS THE IMAGINATION STATION

AUTHOR MARIANNE HERING is the former editor of *Focus on the Family Clubhouse*® magazine. She has written more than a dozen children's books. She likes to read out loud in bed to her fluffy gray-and-white cat, Koshka.

ILLUSTRATOR DAVID HOHN draws and paints books, posters, and projects of all kinds. He works from his studio in Portland, Oregon.

AUTHOR NANCY I. SANDERS is the bestselling and award-winning children's author of more than 80 books. She and her husband, Jeff, like to eat lasagna and sushi. Find out more at *nancyisanders.com*.

FOCUS ᴼᴺ ᵗʜᵉ FAMILY®

No matter who you are, what you're going through, or what challenges your family may be facing, we're here to help. With practical resources —like our toll-free Family Help Line, counseling, and Web sites— we're committed to providing trustworthy, biblical guidance, and support.

Focus on the Family Clubhouse Jr.

Creative stories, fascinating articles, puzzles, craft ideas, and more are packed into each issue of *Focus on the Family Clubhouse Jr.*® magazine. You'll love the way this bright and colorful magazine reinforces biblical values and helps boys and girls (ages 3–7) explore their world. **Subscribe now at** Clubhousejr.com.

Focus on the Family Clubhouse

Through an appealing combination of encouraging content and entertaining activities, *Focus on the Family Clubhouse*® magazine (ages 8–12) will help your children—or kids you care about—develop a strong Christian foundation. **Subscribe now at Clubhousemagazine.com**.